PAPA'S BEDTIME STORY

by Mary Lee Donovan · illustrated by Kimberly Bulcken Root

ALFRED A. KNOPF · NEW YORK

THIS IS A BORZOI BOOK PUBLISHED BY ALFRED A. KNOPF, INC.

Text copyright © 1993 by Mary Lee Donovan
Illustrations copyright © 1993 by Kimberly Bulcken Root
All rights reserved under International and Pan-American Copyright Conventions.
Published in the United States by Alfred A. Knopf, Inc., New York,
and simultaneously in Canada by Random House of Canada Limited, Toronto.
Distributed by Random House, Inc., New York. Book Design by Edward Miller.

Library of Congress Cataloging-in-Publication Data
Donovan, Mary Lee. Papa's bedtime story / by Mary Lee Donovan ;
illustrated by Kimberly Bulcken Root. p.   cm.   Summary: On a warm and
rumbling night in June, a series of human and animal fathers tell bedtime stories
to their children. ISBN 0-679-81790-5 (trade)—ISBN 0-679-91790-X (lib. bdg.)
[1. Bedtime—Fiction. 2. Father and child—Fiction. 3. Animals—Fiction.]
I. Root, Kimberly Bulcken, ill. II. Title. PZ7.D7232Pap 1993
[E]—dc20   91-27792

Manufactured in the United States of America
2   4   6   8   0   9   7   5   3   1

For Mom
and for Dad, who told us
the story of the three cricketeers
—*M. L. D.*

For Barry
—*K. B. R.*

On a warm and rumbling night in June,
there were three peaceful people
in a stout log home
by a big mountain wood
where the air softly blew
through the night and the leaves on the trees.

And the little baby said, in his little baby voice,
"Papa, please tell me a bedtime story."
So Papa began:

On a warm and rumbling night in June,
there were three blinking barn owls
in the safe, sure hold
of an old, proud friend
who had seen many storms
but stood ground in the gale faithfully.

And the little owl said, in his little owl voice,
"Papa, please tell me a bedtime story."
So Papa began:

On a warm and rumbling night in June,
there were three sleepy chipmunks
in a leaf-lined cave
in an old stone wall
'tween a big mountain wood
and a sea made of green timothy.

And the little chipmunk said, in his little chipmunk voice,
"Papa, please tell me a bedtime story."
So Papa began:

On a warm and rumbling night in June,
there were three drowsy rabbits
in a deep earth den
'neath a broad oak tree
in a big mountain wood
where the wind flew about restlessly.

And the little rabbit said, in his little rabbit voice,
"Papa, please tell me a bedtime story."
So Papa began:

On a warm and rumbling night in June,
there were three nodding deer mice
in a smooth, curved nest
lined with long, soft blades
from a wide open field
where the grass rolled and swelled like the sea.

And the little deer mouse said, in his little deer mouse voice,
"Papa, please tell me a bedtime story."
So Papa began:

On a warm and rumbling night in June,
there were three weary crickets
in a small, snug place
where the wind didn't reach
and the rain wouldn't soak,
but a voice could be heard murmuring.

And the little cricket said, in his little cricket voice,
"Papa, please tell me a bedtime story."
So Papa began:

On a warm and rumbling night in June,
there were three joyous wood frogs
in the dark, dark night
and the cool, wet drops
of a sweet summer storm,
and their bells sang of rain and relief.

Then three thousand voices rang in a soothing summer chorus,

"Go to sleep!
Go to sleep!
Go to sleep!"